They Huffed
and
They Puffed

why the three little pigs
chose their buildings

Thomas Rasche

They Huffed and They Puffed

© 2018 Thomas Rasche

Thomas Rasche
Hamilton House, 80 Stokes Croft,
Bristol BS1 3QY, United Kingdom
thomas@rasche.property
www.rasche.property

ISBN 978-0-244-40617-2

Print and distribution by Lulu.com

Front cover: Thomas Rasche.
Back cover: Thomas and Clementine Rasche.

Set in 12pt Sitka Text

Thank you to Edwin Rasche for your comments.

Dedicated to Karen and Clementine.

Contents

Foreword

The need for this book has emerged from the observation that people understand many different things when they talk about 'value'. Using the word, as often as we do, would suggest its meaning is clearly understood. Yet, more often than not, it is a tacit understanding and loaded with assumptions.

Within the context of property, the owners, architects, valuation surveyors, builders, financiers, users, wider community and the literature often do not share an understanding of what 'value' means. Given that property is expensive, involving many people, there should be a clear basis for mutual understanding, so that decisions, costs and effort can be justified. There are many disputes in property, many of which stem from this misunderstanding. This book is intended for the above, as stakeholders and those generally interested in property.

The approach, to writing this as a story book, is with the intention to make the subject compelling and accessible. It is a story based on the Three Little Pigs fable, which gives a context that is familiar, yet also has a property element.

The narrative in this book is set around three ways in which 'value' can be understood, with their associated circumstances, decisions and actions. These understandings draw from sources including architecture (RIBA), surveying (RICS), business literature and my personal observations.

The Definitions chapter is intended to outline meanings of terms used in the book; some having subtle differences. For comparison with conventional or professional definitions, the Further Reading chapter provides additional resources.

Thank you for reading this book. If you have found it to be enjoyable, or it has contributed to discussions and understanding, please share it with others. The definitions are still being debated, so you might have a clearer understanding of what 'value', 'quality' or similarly associated words mean...

Thomas Rasche

Once upon a time...

...there were three little pigs called Declan, Ivory and Quentin. They were happy pigs, living in a comfortable and quiet village between a pond and a forest, about two days' trot away from the seaside. The village was a very desirable place to live for pigs.

During the afternoon of a pleasant spring day, sitting under cherry blossom, the three little pigs were having a conversation. They were wondering how they will plan for the future.

In the conversation, they also discussed a danger they had heard about: there is a wolf that lurks in the nearby forest. They learnt that they have to fear the wolf, as one day, it will surely come to the village where they lived; this was a frightening thought.

They decided that they needed to build themselves some houses...

Declan

Declan was in a hurry and could not afford a complicated building. Knowing this, he went to see Arnold the Architect for advice.

"Arnold", he said, "what is the best advice you can give me for my building?"

"Well," Arnold replied, "I have heard many stories about pigs and wolves, and what you need is a building that keeps you safe when the wolf visits. I suggest you build your house out of bricks."

"Thanks" replied Declan.

"...but I cannot afford to build a brick house."

"Well, it's the only way..."

Then Declan huffed and he puffed and he turned away.

Realising that he needed a different type of material to build his house, Declan began asking other pigs what he could use. He received all sorts of advice including cardboard, corrugated tin, mud and many other suggestions...

The suggestion that Declan thought was best, was to build his house out of straw. Straw was cheap, warm and it was quick to build... perfect!

In no time at all, Declan had ordered the first hay bales of the season from the local farmer and went to work building his straw house. He built it quickly, cheaply, and with a flourish. It had a cockerel shape made of straw on the top of the roof.

"This house is fantastic, everyone will want to live here!" He smiled to himself.

Ivory

Ivory saw what Declan was doing and thought to herself: "why is Declan in such a rush? It doesn't make sense to me; if a building lasts for years and years, he should not build it with so much haste."

Learning from what she saw, she decided to meet Arnold and talk through making a better building.

"Arnold," she started, "I know Declan didn't like your advice, but perhaps you can help me?"

"Sure thing Ivory," he replied, "I'm glad if I can help."

"So, I'm looking for a better building, one that lasts a long time, thereby saving me money on the repair work I will need to do on it.

"Oh," she continued, "I say that, but I don't have much more money than Declan."

With this, Arnold's brow furrowed; he was thinking about how he should reply.

"I understand what you are saying," began Arnold, "but the reality is, that the best advice I can give you is that you build a house out of bricks."

"Thank you" replied Ivory.

"...but I cannot afford to build a brick house."

"Well, it's the only way..."

With that, Ivory huffed and she puffed and she turned away.

"Surely there's a better way to build than with flimsy straw..." grumbled Ivory.

To find a solution, she began doing research and read all the books in the local library on the subject. She read all afternoon and only left the library when it was time to close.

Ivory was thinking to herself as she patted along the path on her way home one day. "I need a material I can afford, but that will not be as flimsy as straw, something that will stick around for longer." She pondered.

She considered her options, with all the building materials she had read about earlier. But which one of the many materials is suitable?

Then she stopped suddenly, as she realised what she had said to herself: "...something that will stick around for longer."...That's it! A stick house, that will stick around for longer!

The following week Ivory (who is never in a rush), went to see the manager of the local copse. She ordered large bundles of long, flexible and rather beautiful willow sticks to be delivered to where she wanted to build her house.

With a cheerful wave, the manager delivered the large stick bundles for Ivory. They were bound together as wide as barrels, which is just about a manageable size.

Ivory began building her house. It being willow, she was able to weave the sticks in and out and in between each other.

"This will make the house longer lasting, so that should a stick break, the other sticks will keep holding it in place."

It took two months of careful work for Ivory to finish her house. By the end, she was very pleased and proud of it.

"Living in this house, you'd never want to leave it!"

Quentin

Quentin was an observant pig. He trotted around with his nose in the air, not on the ground, so unlike other pigs. He would smell the air around him, but more importantly, this way he could see what was going on in the village. He was a costume cutter, a pig that made fine clothes. He liked meeting and talking to the other pigs, hearing their opinions, and seeing what they chose to wear.

It will be of no surprise to you, that he knew of Declan and Ivory's houses. He saw where they were and what they were doing. He was so well informed in fact, that it was almost as if he had overhead every conversation they had with Arnold. He knew, that it had to be a brick house that he builds, there's just no alternative.

"Arnold!" called Quentin, when he passed the studio, "how nice to bump into you by chance."

Actually, he had planned this, so it wasn't really a chance bump.

"I was meaning to ask you," Quentin looked at Arnold directly, "could you help me? I wish to build a house and I want to build it with bricks."

"Yes Quentin, I'd be happy to help you," replied Arnold.

"But if I can ask you, why do you want a brick house?" Arnold spoke quietly, "I mean, all the other pigs haven't listened to me, so how come you want to do this?"

"Ah," replied Quentin sniffing the air, "we all need a house that is protection against the wolf, and I don't want to be in a house that's not good enough. You recommended a brick house, and as you are the expert, I believe you."

This was a good reply, and Arnold was confident that Quentin meant what he said.

"That's great to hear," answered Arnold, "but then I have a question before we can proceed..."

"Yes?"

"A brick house is more expensive, can you afford a brick house?" This was an important question that needed to be asked at the beginning, so that there was no confusion once the building work starts.

Quentin huffed and he puffed and he stuttered, "Hmm, well..., err..."

"Let me ask the large sow at the bank, she will help me answer the question for you." Quentin turned around so as to trot back to the high street. With a determined voice, he called back: "I will be back soon with an answer."

No more than a day later, Quentin returned to see Arnold.

"I have been to see Tilly!" he announced as he paraded into Arnold's office. Tilly was the sow at the bank.

"That's great, I hope it is good news," came the reply from beyond a huge table, piled high with technical drawings.

"Yes it is. I have the money, so work can begin!"

And so it was, that Arnold began designing a brick house for Quentin. He made plans, ordered a pile of bricks and had a bricklayer come to his parcel of land. Work began with strings marking where the walls were to be, the mixing of mud and the stacking of bricks.

As work proceeded, Quentin imagined where he would eat his apple pies and where he would seat his guests; how the sun will shine through the windows and how it would be warm in the winter.

With a finished brick house, Quentin hosted a party, inviting Arnold as the special guest, having designed such a fine house. Quentin will be happy living in this brick house.

The visit

It wasn't just Quentin who was observing the goings-on in the village... In the nearby forest, there was a wolf watching what was happening beyond the edge of the forest. The wolf is big and scary, with sharp teeth and bright starey eyes.

This wolf was not just watching, he was planning how to take advantage of the changes he saw happening in the village. Three delicious looking pigs would be perfect for his rumbling tummy. These three pigs had built the new houses that he now wants to investigate...

In the depth of night and with a faint rustle of leaves, the wolf tiptoed past the edge of the forest, down towards the village. As he passes the familiar old houses, he hears snoring and zzzz's. His starlit shadow slips past these houses and on towards the newly built ones. His jaws are watering and his tongue hangs low as the houses come into view.

As the wolf approached the straw house, he reached out to knock on the door.

He calls out to the pig inside: "Little pig, little pig, let me in; I'm a hungry old wolf and I need my din'!"

"Eek, eek" came the reply from within, "I'll not let you in!"

So then the wolf took a deep breath and blew the house down... now his stomach has a filling.

The wolf moved on, through the night; he has much more in his sights. The wolf approaches the stick house, sticking out a claw to press the doorbell: "Little pig, little pig, let me in; I'm a hungry old wolf and I need my din'!"

There was a flurry of activity: "Eek, eek" came the reply from within, "I'll not let you in!"

So the wolf took a deep breath and blew right through the house... how he enjoyed this second helping.

Again, the wolf moves on. This time, he is moving towards the brick house. As the house looms over the wolf, he taps persistently on the window: "Little pig, little pig, let me in; I'm a hungry old wolf and I need my din'!"

Quentin's voice called from inside: "Eek, eek; I'll not let you in!"

"Well then, I'll take a deep breath and blow your house down," roars the wolf.

With that, he took a deep breath and blew and blew... but he cannot blow the brick house down.

The wolf huffed and he puffed and murmured: "well, my tummy is brimming." With that, the wolf passed back through the village and went back up to the dark forest from where he had come.

The town meets

The village awoke to the news of the wolf's visit in the night. As you can imagine, there was a lot of commotion. A village meeting was called, to talk about what had happened, to which everyone was invited.

Arnold raised the problem of choosing the wrong building materials. The wolf had blown down the house made of straw, and through the house made of sticks. Clearly then, everyone should be building with bricks!

However, others did not see it this way. They talked about fences and ditches, alarms and even chopping down the forest. Arnold was barely even heard.

Clearly, there was no simple answer, so the town resolved to discuss it again at a future meeting...

On the way out, after the meeting had finished, Arnold bumped into Declan, who was in a rush as usual. "Declan, sorry to hear about your straw house," he started, "...and by the way, how did you manage to survive the wolf's visit? I thought he blew your house down and ate all within?"

"Oh, thanks Arnold, yes it is a shame about the house I built." He replied, continuing: "...and the wolf did devour all within, which is a terrible story to recount."

"But, you didn't end up as the wolf's meal?"

"Oh no. You see, I built the house to sell to somebody else."

"Really? So you weren't in the house last night?"

"No I wasn't."

Arnold was puzzled, it didn't make too much sense to him.

"As you know," mentioned Declan, "I am in a rush."

"Yes, I have noticed."

"Well, the reason is, I put all the money I have towards building the house, so I had nothing left." Declan was explaining, "Therefore, I need the house to be built quickly, so that I can sell it and get my money back."

"I understand," replied Arnold, "...otherwise you'll go hungry for too long?"

"Yes."

"This explains why you are rushing," continued Arnold, "but why did you choose a straw house rather than a solid brick house?"

Declan answered in a matter-of-fact voice: "It was good value. A straw house is good enough."

"Good enough?"

"Yes. It's good enough to sell."

Arnold understood. "Good enough to sell...hmm. But not good enough for when the wolf visits."

"Had you suggested that you can design a house that is inexpensive to build, with the added value that it will sell easily and at a high price, I would have employed you...."

With that, Declan rushed off.

Amongst the daffodils

Arnold trotted off towards the village green. He wanted a rest, to sit amongst the daffodils and think about both the wolf's visit and the design of the straw house. "I couldn't possibly design a straw house, knowing it's not solid enough for when the wolf visits" he was thinking.

As Arnold moved between the tufts of grass, a friendly and gentle voice called over to him.

"Hello Arnold."

Arnold looked up. He recognised the voice, it was Ivory.

"Hello Ivory," he called. "I am surprised to see you! Didn't your stick house get blown to shreds and the wolf eat all there-in?"

"Well, it was my stick house, yes." She replied as she ambled closer. "It is a terrible thing that has happened, but it wasn't me inside the house."

"Oh, that's a surprise... that's similar to Declan's situation, whom I spoke to earlier today." Arnold considered it strange that the same thing also happened to Ivory, "did you also sell your house?"

"No, I didn't sell my house," she furrowed her brow at the thought. "I think long-term, I think that time is on my side; I'm a value investor."

"So you keep the house but don't live in it?"

"Yes Arnold, I rent it out." Ivory replied. "Over a long period of time, I have been saving my money, which I used to build my house. I had enough money to buy nice willow sticks to build the house."

"But, if you are so careful with your money, why not build a brick house?" asked Arnold.

"I couldn't afford a brick house, and anyway, willow is a good material. Over time, willow does not need maintenance, so I can make the most of a return by renting out my house. I will be able to put the money back into my savings. Even after the wolf's visit, the house will be easy to fix."

Having reflected on Declan's earlier comment, Arnold suggested: "let me ask you: would you have let me design a house for you, had I suggested you need willow, not bricks?"

"Maybe," replied Ivory, slowly turning to the side, "had you offered to design me a long-lasting and easy to maintain house, then definitely."

"So it's not about the bricks, or sticks, themselves, but how long you want your house to last?"

"Exactly." Ivory replied softly.

"But what about the protection from the wolf, where only bricks will do?"

"It is true that bricks will protect my house from the wolf, I can see now why you suggested it. But, it is not what I wanted; it is also too expensive."

Quentin's opinion

Arnold sat on a bench, watching Ivory as she drifted away; she had a lot to sort out, given that her stick house had gaping holes in it. "It's all about cost and time," he thought to himself. "Is that it? Is safety and risk not more important?" These thoughts felt uncomfortable to him, so he decided to talk to someone he knew thought differently. Arnold went to see Quentin.

Quentin was enjoying the dappled shade under the canopy that Arnold had designed for him.

"Hi Quentin."

"Hello Arnold, how are you?"

"Quentin, I have a few questions to ask you..."

"Sure, ask away."

"I have spoken to Declan and Ivory about the cost of their buildings, the choice of building materials, their timeframe, but also safety if the wolf visits. You were visited by the wolf last night, wouldn't you say that security is the most important thing in a building?"

"Oh yes, that's why I liked your suggestion to build in brick," replied Quentin while raising his snout towards the horizon.

"...but it's also much more than that."

"More? ...does it include both the timing and cost that Declan and Ivory were talking about?"

"Yes, all these things matter. But, it's the whole picture, or gestalt as I call it. It is the inclusion of all these things. I also share your values."

Quentin took a deep breath to try to explain.

"Arnold, you are an architect, you bring so much to a building: you ask me what is important, making it nice for me to live in it."

"Yes, that goes without saying. Of course I design with you in mind," replied Arnold.

"The thing that we decided was most important to me, was security from the wolf..."

"...so we chose bricks, yes..." Arnold interrupted.

"...yes, but I also had to be able to use it well, to work here and make the money to pay for the bricks in the first place..."

Quentin paused, before he continued, "...but even more, you also built it to look and feel nice."

"I remember our discussions, we thought carefully about all these things; we made sure we got the priorities right first time."

"And that," continued Quentin, "is something else you brought: you knew how to get the best out of the design process." Quentin looked up to the canopy above him, "it has ended up being of value to me, even though the bricks were expensive. Our time and money was not wasted, because we gave it enough thought and preparation.

"And look" Quentin sniffed, "it's a wonderful space and I'm proud of it."

Arnold gave an approving sigh, "It is...architecture!"

Arnold's notes

Arnold went home to make some notes; he wanted to prepare for the next town meeting. He needed to be able to explain why brick houses are best. He also needed to make sense of the different comments he had heard from Declan, Ivory and Quentin.

He caught his reflection in a mirror as he passed through the door.

"A brick house really has a value worth paying," he said to himself, "but not everyone sees this... they understand value to be something else..."

With these words, Arnold sat down to write down the meaning of 'value'. He also flipped through his dictionary to double-check the definitions. Actually, when he looked in the dictionary, and thought about it more, there seemed to be a few different meanings, so he ended up with these notes:

Arnold's notes

Declan's values are about *price*, the amount of money someone will pay to buy the house. He was also worried about the *expense* to build. *Profit* is the difference between these, calculated as:

$$\text{profit} = \text{price} - \text{expense}$$

Ivory's values are about the *return*, or the *investment value*. The return on an investment is the amount of money that is earned, or returned, each year. This is also called the *interest*, or a *yield* if it's a percentage. Money needs to be available to make the investment, which is called the *capital*. The capital expense to build can be justified, if the yield is good, calculated as:

$$\text{yield\%} = \frac{\text{return per year}}{\text{capital}}$$

Quentin's values are about *worth*, the various benefits that he will enjoy, after considering the various costs (e.g. time, money, hassle etc.). The calculation for this is similar to Declan's, but also considers the non-financial values:

$$\text{worth} = \text{benefits} - \text{costs}$$

The origin of the word value is *valere*, from Latin meaning 'to be worth'. Depending on context, value can mean price, worth or cost. It can be a person's opinion, or the market's opinion. It can refer to financial (tangible) and/or non-financial (intangible) values. It can be calculated as an absolute figure, or a subjective estimate, as well as an amount that changes with time.

The following day, Arnold looked at his notes again. The notes seemed useful, but he still had his doubts about something...

"Quentin made an *appraisal*..."

Arnold had found the word 'appraisal' in the dictionary, meaning it is Quentin's personal and subjective opinion of worth. This is different to a 'valuation', which means the selling price on the market.

"...so what does this appraisal of Quentin's look like? ...and how come Tilly was willing to give him so much money, enough to pay for a brick house?"

With this question in mind, Arnold set off to see Tilly.

At the bank

Arnold arrived at the bank and sat patiently in the waiting room for Tilly the sow. He had his notes on a floppy sheet of paper in front of him.

Tilly arrived as if on tip-toes, she floated in to greet him. She had large, round and thick-rimmed glasses balanced at the top of her snout. She also had a voice that sounded a bit squeaky, just like a door hinge needing oil.

"How can I help you?" she squeaked kindly.

Arnold began by explaining the conversations he had had with Declan, Ivory and Quentin. Then he talked about the wolf's visit and how terrible that was. Finally, he presented his notes to her, explaining that he understood the differences between all three of them, but still didn't understand why Quentin managed to afford his brick house.

"I see you have given it some thought...". She paused before she continued, "you understand what Ivory was doing: she had money, and she invested this in a stick house?"

"Yes, I understand that" Arnold was clear about that.

"At the bank, we call that an *asset*, it is something that earns you a return."

Arnold then suggested: "if Ivory built a good quality house, it will last for years earning her a return for a long time. She built an asset."

"Now, Declan had the opposite problem. He was losing money because his capital, the money he started with, was stuck while he was building."

"He was losing money?" Arnold asked, "he was only paying for the straw which he need."

"That's right, he was losing money by doing that."

Arnold didn't quite get it, because Declan was putting his money into his house. He wasn't losing money, was he? He sat silently hoping Tilly would continue and explain.

"He had what I call an *opportunity cost*. In other words, he could have earned a return by leaving his money with me at the bank, but he chose not to. His cost is his lost opportunity of earning an alternative return."

"He was missing out."

"Yes, he was missing out on an opportunity, so this can be thought of as a cost." Tilly took a breath, wondering if Arnold's expression meant he was understanding, or that he was confused.

"If something loses money, we call that a *liability*."

"Declan's house was a liability?" Arnold tested the idea by speaking it out.

"Yes, and that is why he is always in a rush. While his house was being built, it was a liability, so he wants to move on to sell it as quickly as he could."

There was a pause, while Tilly studied Arnold's sheet of paper again.

"If I remember correctly, your question was why Quentin managed to borrow more money off me, compared to the others?"

"That's right, yes."

"Well, the answer is that he created value."

"Value? What do you mean by value?" Arnold wanted to be clear about this...

"To be exact, investment value."

"Like Ivory?"

"Kind of. You see, Ivory started with money, which she used to build an asset, which earns a return." Tilly looked up, then across to the picture of Australian kangaroos on her wall. "...except Quentin did the opposite, he did it upside down."

"Upside down?!" Arnold thought this to be an odd thing to say. "What do you mean?"

"To explain again, Ivory went 'from money, to an asset, to a return'. By contrast, Quentin went from 'a return, to an asset, to money'."

"Haha, upside down? You mean back to front?" Arnold chortled.

"Quentin showed me how he would be earning money, by being able to create beautiful clothes if he had a nice brick building. In terms of the flow of his day-to-day money, making regular earnings is the same as making regular returns."

"So how does regular money then get converted to an asset, so you then give him more money?"

"Simply, if you add up all the day-to-day money (which incidentally we call *cashflow*), you end up with a big amount. That big amount of money is how much investment value he brings.

That figure is the money I offered him so that he could build his house..."

"...and his house is his asset." Arnold finished her sentence.

"That is correct. I am glad you have understood this." Tilly then continued: "This is a bit more technical, but to work it out this way round, we do a calculation, we *capitalise* his earnings, to then establish the asset value. To calculate this, we transpose, or swap, Ivory's formula around so that we can calculate the capital like this..." she then wrote out Arnold's formula slightly differently:

$$\text{capital} = \frac{\text{return per year}}{\text{yield\%}}$$

Arnold smiled, "I see why you say it's upside down!"

He was happy with what he now understood and reached to get his notes back.

There was a long pause...

"Wait a minute," he said, looking over his notes, "this isn't the same formula that I had for Quentin. Does that mean my formula is wrong?"

"No, it's not wrong; it shows something different." She reassured Arnold.

"Different?"

"Yes, when Quentin talks about his building, what does he talk about when he mentions value?"

"He talks about security, comfort and being able to sew."

"Exactly."

"Exactly?" Arnold did not understand.

"Quentin talks about *non-financial benefits* to you, which is why you created a formula like you did. With me, he talked about the money he will be earning, which is all about *financial benefits*."

"Hmm, they are really different then, aren't they?"

"Yes they are." confirmed Tilly.

"However, it is important to recognise, that Quentin needed both financial *and* non-financial values for his building."

"Is there a clear way that I can describe this distinction, the two differences that we are talking about? Quentin talks about using the house for many things, that help him earn, whereas you look directly at how he has made use of the house for money."

"That is a good question." replied Tilly. "I see many people who talk about how they will make use of a house, as well as how much money they will make. So I have two words to distinguish these uses more clearly:"

"The first is *use* value. This is the financial side, the return or earnings that can be made; Quentin earns money directly from his sewing."

Tilly then made a gesture to the side. "The second is *utility* value. These are the benefits of using the building that affect the finances, but not directly; these are intangible benefits, important things like security from the wolf, comfort, but also that there is sufficient light through the windows so that Quentin can sew."

"I understand," confirmed Arnold, "Quentin sees the worth of his brick house, which its 'utility value'..."

"Yes" she responded encouragingly.

"...but he spoke to you about its 'use value' clarifying what money he can earn."

Tilly smiled.

Arnold concluded: "So, Quentin had both: use value *and* utility value. And, because you saw that he had both of these, you were able to help him finance his house."

Tilly was now nodding proudly, seeing that Arnold had understood.

"Oh, and there is one more thing I can show you," Tilly tiptoed over to her cabinet and brought over a sheet of paper with notes written on them, set out in a neat grid.

"These are my notes that I refer to, which are the things I look out for. There are similarities to your notes, as well as to the things that we have talked about."

With that, she scribbled the names of Declan, Ivory and Quentin on her sheet and presented it to him →

"Thank you for this," said Arnold, "I will study this with interest."

With that, the meeting came to a close. Arnold stood up, thanked Tilly for her time and left.

Declan Ivory Quentin

Investor	Capital-	Value-	Quality-
Property developer	Merchant-	Investment-	Owner Occupier
Building purpose	Buy and sell	Buy and hold	Buy and use
Business plan	Building as a product to sell at a profit.	Property asset rented out for long term.	A business location, to operate & grow.
Financial plan	Increase Capital value.	Yield; a return on Capital	Create revenue, which is then capitalised
Finance calculations	price $-$ expense $=$ profit	yield% $= \dfrac{\text{return}}{\text{capital}}$	$\dfrac{\text{return}}{\text{yield\%}} =$ capital
Non-finance calculations			benefits $-$ costs $=$ worth
Time	Fast: cost of capital is a liability	Slow: long term revenue is an asset	Timespan of business interest
Change-ability	No flexibility required over the short term	Flexibility and options for changes in use	Resilience to uncertainty: business and values change.
Process	Simple and fast process	Durability and maintenance considerations	Many values to consider, so careful design consideration
Rules of thumb	Buy as cheap as possible. Exit (sell) as soon as possible.	Seek a long term, low risk return, i.e. a *use value.*	It has to feel right. Both *use-* and *utility values* are needed.

A change of mind

Arnold realised that he had to accept each of Declan, Ivory and Quentin's perspectives. They had values, and they stayed consistent with each of these.

Arnold was strangely satisfied. Now, he would not suggest the best solution straight away. He knew better: he has to ask and find out about his customer's values.

"If I ask the right questions and listen to them, I will understand and be better able to work with anyone..."

This sounded good to Arnold...
...but then he shook his head.

"No, I won't do that" he disagreed with himself.

Arnold squinted as he looked across to the outline of Quentin's house in the distance.

"I think that Declan and Ivory huffed and puffed and walked away from me, because my values don't align with their values; they spotted it immediately. We might understand each other, but that doesn't mean we can work well together. It's not a good fit: I will always want to make choices that are like Tilly's Quality Investor, yet they will always assume that I should do it differently...

"I believe that quality is value."

Arnold raised his snout as high as Quentin does, and he called out determinedly: "I shall continue to build brick houses!"

The town decides

A week has passed and the townsfolk have called another meeting to talk again about the wolf's visit. This is an urgent matter, so they are looking for solutions. On the agenda are the horrible wolf, the tragic loss and the three houses.

"Everybody, we have a wolf problem, what shall we do about it?" asked the Chief Councillor, who was chairing the meeting.

Declan was first to lift his trotter, "I suggest, that if we buy a fence machine, we can build ourselves a cheap protective fence around the village. Further, we can set up a fence company, which will grow and make more fences to sell to neighbouring villages."

Ivory decided to respond. She stood up slowly, "it is important to have a solution that will last a long time. A fence is too basic, I am not convinced it will last a long time." She then continued "...worse, a proper solution will be expensive, and yet I cannot see how we can get a return on our investment."

Arnold stood up to comment, emboldened by what he had learned, "if we build a good barrier, we will get a return on our investment: a utility value in the form of security. We can't easily put a price on it, but it is very important and valuable to us.

"However, as Ivory stated, a fence will not be long lasting enough. What we need therefore, is to build a wall out of bricks, because bricks are quality."

With this, everyone in the room shook their heads, they huffed and they puffed.

As the room went silent, Arnold lowered himself into his seat. He was somewhat confused with everyone's response.

At last, Quentin commented, "Thank you Arnold for your suggestion.

Can I ask, what exactly do you mean by 'bricks are quality'?"

"Bricks are a solid material" Arnold replied.

"To me, that's a bit confusing, because that's not what we want," Quentin replied, "the solidness of bricks refers to its substance, its intrinsic value, if you like."

"Intrinsic value?" Arnold wanted to understand what Quentin meant.

"Yes, the intrinsic value is what *it is*, the material properties of the bricks, the effort to make them etc.

"By contrast, we want protection, which is what *it does*, the extrinsic value."

Arnold clarified: "I see... what I suppose I mean is the *value* of bricks, not their *quality*, is in their ability to be secure; or, as you might understand it, their extrinsic value. I did not mean to suggest a signature wall made of bricks, just because bricks are a good quality material."

Arnold recognised that with hindsight, this had applied to all of

Declan, Ivory and Quentin's buildings. They had all sought extrinsic value in their buildings.

"Anyway, bricks are far too expensive!" Declan interjected.

Tilly from the bank raised a squeak, "yes, bricks are expensive... too expensive. I am sure we can find an alternative material that will function well and provide our security. We have the problem that the protection will cost us, but we will not be able to earn that money back."

The Chief Councillor invited different suggestions, for materials that may solve the security issue: "So far, we have fencing, which is cheap and fast, but not long lasting, and then we have brick, which is too expensive. Are there any other suggestions?"

A few different ideas were discussed, but then Ivory raised her hand. "I have a suggestion," she offered.

"Ivory, yes, please speak."

"This may seem like a different kind of solution, but what about a hedgerow? A hedgerow will grow and provide us with security, with minimum new materials.

"What a great idea!" Arnold called out. There was nodding around the room.

"I have heard that the laying of hedgerows can be very secure, and I love the appearance of hawthorn and elder," offered Quentin.

The Chief Councillor agreed, "this seems to be the best solution so far, with many benefits."

Tilly stood up and offered her comment. "I would say that a hedgerow is affordable because of low capital costs to start with, but there will be high ongoing maintenance costs. A hedgerow is not a financial investment, nor is it a growing business (even though the hedge itself grows); it will not generate any money."

"A not-for-profit hedge *and* ideally a not-for-loss hedge too!" joked Declan.

"Yes, I agree," the Chief Councillor responded quickly, with a hint of a smile. "This is possible, we can manage the hedge as a community company; we can allow it to operate as a not-for-profit like that. As it is so important to us all, we will pay for it from our taxes. We can use the opportunity to hire our local workers too."

All the pigs in the room agreed that this seemed a good solution.

Arnold agreed to plan where the hedgerows will run and to coordinate the skilled workers.

And so it was that a secure hedgerow was built surrounding the village. The pigs in the village were able to live securely and happily ever after.

Definitions

Appraisal, a personal or subjective assessment of value, expressed in financial terms. A price is put on all the (*in*-) *tangible values*: both financial <u>and</u> non-financial. See *best value*. Contrast with *valuation*.

Asset, an item earning money. It appears in the financial *Balance Sheet*.

Benefits, the *financial* <u>and</u> *non-financial* advantages that are enjoyed. These can be *tangible*, *intangible*, subjective or objective e.g. *time*, *cost*, *quality*, impact, finance, adaptability, likability, enjoyment, socially- /environmentally sustainable, *functionality*, and many more. See also *value*.

Budget, an amount of money with a ceiling limit, or target, available for a particular purpose; a plan. The limit of affordability.

Capital, an amount of money, a lump sum for *investment*. Capital = *equity* + *debt*.

Capitalise, the *Capital* value equivalent of future *revenues*. See also *NPV*, *LLC*, *WLC*.

Cashflow, the cash going in and out. It excludes money you have earned but not received payment for yet.

Changeability, change in context or situation.

> **Risk**, the expected changes and day-to-day 'noise', the variability.

> **Uncertainty**, the large, unpredictable changes in *value* and circumstances over time. Systemic & non-systemic.

Costs, the financial <u>and</u> non-financial disadvantages that apply.

Debt, your borrowed money.

Discounting, calculation to adjust future income and expenses, so as to *capitalise* these, accounting for inflation and *risk*, at a certain rate. See *LLC*, *NPV*, *WLC*, *valuation*.

Expense, the financial cost.

Extrinsic (Quality- or **Value-)**, see *extrinsic value*.

Financial statements, summary of finances, as snapshots in time:

> **Cashflow Statement**, immediate and short term finances.

Profit and Loss Statement, or **P&L**, medium term, annual finances.
Balance Sheet, long term finances.

Function, aka performance, see *extrinsic value*.

Income, the money earned.

Intangible (-value or **-benefits)**, the subjective, difficult to define, transient or elusive values. E.g. social value, culture, brand, wellbeing etc. Their character is often scalable, easily copied, mutually complementary, but difficult to justify financially.

Interest, the annual financial *return* from an *asset*. It can be expressed as a percentage *yield*.
Simple interest, the same *return* every year relative to an amount of *capital*.
Compound interest, each interest payment is reinvested to increase the *capital*.

Investment, *capital* is put into an *asset* and earns a *return*, from income (*investment value*, e.g. Ivory) or growth (*quality investment*, e.g. Quentin).

Intrinsic (Quality- or **Value-)**, see *intrinsic value*.

Liability, an item that loses money. It appears on the financial *Balance Sheet*.

Life Cycle Costs (LLC), the *capitalised* value of future property *expenses*, within a business interest timeframe, including maintenance and refurbishments. *WLC*.

Loss, the same as *profit*, but as a negative number.

Net Present Value (NPV), the *Capital* value equivalent of net future *revenues*, after *expenses*, at today's *prices*. Future revenue is *discounted*.

Non-financial values are about *intangibles*, *utility value* and *benefits* without direct financial impact.

Opportunity cost, the *worth* (net *benefits*) foregone, of the next best alternative. Usually considered in financial terms.

pa = per annum, i.e. per year.

Price, the amount of money exchanged, when something is bought/sold. See *market value*.

Process, the decision making and activity during the development time, such as procuring a building: both design and build.

Profit, as *financial values* only: the net *income*, after *expenses* have been deducted. See also *financial statement*.

Purpose, see *extrinsic value*.

Quality, the ability to meet or exceed expectations. Different uses include:

  Quality, precious, desirable, attractive or exclusive.

  Quality (value), used synonymously for various meanings of *value*, including: *value feature*, *benefit-*, *gestalt-*, *intrinsic-*, *extrinsic-*, *investment-* and *affordable value*.

  Quality Investment, an *asset* with a future of financial growth: as *worth*, *value* or business *return*. An investment with predictable and long term *returns*, low *risk* and less downside *uncertainty*. See also *investment*. Contrast with *investment value*.

Return, total money gained, or realised, from an investment after a period of time.

Revenue, the gross *income* earned annually.

Risk, day-to-day volatility or noise. See *changeability*.
  Risk premium, a higher *discount* rate reflecting higher risks.

Tangible (-value or –benefits), what can be seen, itemised, counted and people perceive equally; it can be quantified or counted e.g. finance.

Time changes things. *Value* can be better understood considering timespans, e.g. the business interest, or those of the different *financial statements*. Some terms are understood within timeframes, e.g. *asset, liability, cashflow, yield* and *capitalisation.* Extended or constrained time impacts *value*, e.g. depreciation and *discounting. Emergent value* appears with time: social currency becomes social capital, culture becomes cultural capital, space becomes place, *intrinsic value* becomes *extrinsic value*, PR becomes a brand. Heritage has Institutional Value.

Uncertainty, see *changeability*.

Value, used with many different meanings:
> **Value (a measure)**, a measure of *benefit*:
>> **Value (Absolute-, or quantity)**, a financial figure, other unit or number, e.g. gross- or net value, *market value*, *price* or *capital*.
>>
>> **Value (Relative-)**, quantified in terms of comparison, to have 'better value'. Ordinal ranking for comparison, or Cardinal ranking includes weighting
>
> **Value (a feature)**, meaning a functional feature, an *intrinsic* or *quality* characteristic.
>
> **Value (Added-)**, the *benefits* added to a product or service, such as *use-* and *utility value*, so that a client or customer sees an increase in *worth*.
>
> **Value (Affordable-, or Cheap-)**, an inexpensive amount or *value measure*, within a *budget*, or a relatively low *price*.
>
> **Value (Benefit-)**, see *benefits*.
>
> **Value (Best-,Worst-,Maximal-,Maximin-, Minimax-)**. The results of an *appraisal*. These labels arise from decision theory: Maximal value (a no

less satisfactory choice), minimax
(likely lowest maximum value),
maximin (maximum value of
minimum outcomes) etc. See *value
measure*.

Value chain, same *gestalt-* and *process
values* mapped onto various scales,
stages and levels of production.

Value (Emergent- or **Process-)**, within
the culture and use over time.
Emergent complexity as an adaptive
system. An *added-* and *benefit value*,
a response to *changeability*.

Value (Extrinsic-), aka *function* or
purpose. The external effect, impact,
or ability to meet/exceed functional
requirements and *benefits*, both
financial and non-financial. Including
appearance, security, durability,
utility value and *use value*.

Value (Financial-), is about money.

Value (Gestalt- or **Institutional-)**, the
balance and trade-offs in choices,
design and *value features*. Value that
is more than the sum of the parts, to
become something of *worth*, an
expression of culture and *values*. The

embodiment of a value typology: a chosen set of *benefits.* A brand. For example, the priorities between *time*, *cost* and *quality*.

Value (Intrinsic-), the characteristics, such as the technical features, surface, material, substance, durability, workmanship, effort and other embodied qualities.

Value (Intangible-), see *intangible*.

Value (Investment- or **Income-)**, an *asset* that has a predictable *revenue* stream. This can be *capitalised* into a *value quantity*. See also *investment* and *valuation*. Contrast with *quality investment*.

Value Management, the focus on *values*, *added value* and *value proposition*, to increase net financial value. Related is value engineering, also aiming to increase net financial value, but has a focus to reduce cost and production efficiencies.

Value (Market-), the (likely) exchange *price* in an open and transparent market.

Value (Non-financial-), an undefined/-able amount or quantity of *benefit*, or something *intangible*, e.g. social value, cultural value, knowledge...

Value (Optimal-), ideal or best choice.

Value proposition, the *worth* of a service offered to a client, having *added value*. Described in financial and non-financial terms.

Value ratio, the *price* to *function* ratio.

Value (Scale-), impact of scale change, including negative marginal utility or positive economies of scale.

Value (Tangible-), see *tangible*.

Value (Use-), the *financial value* of using the property or object.

Value (Utility-), an indirect, *intangible* impact on financial value. See also *non-financial value*.

Values (Belief-), your core values, ethics, principles, moral code and/or standards that drive your opinions and actions. These will be expressed as a *Gestalt value*, or *Institutional value*.

Valuation, an objective assessment of *price*, usually a *market value* at a particular date. Three methods to calculate this:

Comparison to other similar building *prices*, to inform a *value*.

Investment value is calculated by *capitalisation*, e.g. *NPV*. See also *investment*.

Procurement cost is sometimes used to value (an unusual) building. This is comparable to an asset's face value. Contrast with *appraisal*.

Whole Life Costs (WLC), the *capitalised* value of future property expenses, within a business interest timeframe, as with *LLC*, but also includes the user, owner and financing aspects. Embodied cost, demolition and disposal also considered.

Worth means the net *benefits*, after *costs* are considered, both financially <u>and</u> non-financially. By comparison, the worth as financial only is 'net value'; see also *valuation, investment value, market value, NPV* and *profit*.

Yield, a percentage relationship between the annual *interest* earned relative to *capital*.

Further reading

Armatys, J, Askham, P and Green, M (2009) *Principles of Valuation*. London: Estates Gazette.

Dallas, MF (2011) *Value And Risk Management*. Oxford: Blackwell Publishing.

Haskel, H and Westlake, S (2017) *Capitalism without Capital: The Rise of the Intangible Economy*. Princeton: Princeton University Press.

HM Treasury (2011) *The Green Book: Appraisal and Evaluation in Central Government*. London: LSO

Kelly, J, Male, S and Graham, D (2015). *Value Management of Construction Projects*. Second ed. Chichester: Wiley Blackwell.

Kiyosaki, RT (1997) *Rich Dad Poor Dad.* London: Time Warner Paperbacks.

Macmillan, S (2003) *Designing Better Buildings: Quality and Value in the Built Environment*. Abingdon: Routledge.

Osterwalder, Pigneur, Bernarda, Smith and Papadakos (2014) *Value Proposition Design*. Hoboken: John Wiley & Sons.

Patel, R (2011) *The Value of Nothing*. London: Portobello Books.

Rasche, T (2016) *Concepts of Value in Property*. Raleigh: Lulu.com.

Rasche, T (2016) *Strategic Definition – Property Development Workbook*. Raleigh: Lulu.com. Available from: www.lulu.com

RIBA (2013) *Plan of Work 2013*. London: Royal Institute of British Architects. Available from: www.architecture.com

RICS (2016) *RICS Valuation - Global Standards 2017*. The *RICS Red Book*. London: Royal Institution of Chartered Surveyors.

UKGBC (2018) Reports: *Social Value in New Development*, and *Capturing the Value of Sustainability*. Available from www.ukgbc.org

Warner, S and Hussain, S (2017) *The Finance Book*. Harlow: Pearson Education.

VALiD (2015) *Value in Design (VALiD) Framework*. Source: www.valueindesign.com

About the author

Thomas Rasche graduated in Architecture RIBA parts I&II from the University of Liverpool in 1994. In 2016 he graduated with a Master of Science in Real Estate Finance and Investment from the University of the West of England.

His thesis investigated the alignment of values between valuation surveyors and architects. Subsequent work includes the publications *Concepts of Value in Property* and *Strategic Definition – Property Development Workbook*.

Architecturally, he has designed and managed a variety of buildings types and scales, from large public buildings and commercial properties to private dwellings.

Thomas has worked in the UK, Germany and Ireland; he now lives in Bristol.

Form follows value;
value follows form.